A TEENY TINY BABY

AMY SCHWARTZ

ORCHARD BOOKS • NEW YORK

Orchard Books
95 Madison Avenue
New York, NY 10016

Manufactured in the United States of America
Printed by Barton Press, Inc.
Bound by Horowitz/Rae
Book design by Mina Greenstein

The text of this book is set in 18 point Weiss.
The illustrations are rendered in gouache and reproduced in full color.

10   9   8   7   6   5   4   3   2

Library of Congress Cataloging-in-Publication Data
Schwartz, Amy.
A teeny tiny baby / by Amy Schwartz.
p.   cm. "A Richard Jackson book"—Half t.p.
Summary: A baby describes the many activities he
enjoys, both at home and out in the busy city.
ISBN 0-531-06818-8.   ISBN 0-531-08668-2 (lib. bdg.)
[1. Babies—Fiction.   2. City and town life—Fiction.]   I. Title.
PZ7.S406Te   1994   [E]—dc20   93-4876

For Jacob Henry,
who used to be
a teeny tiny baby

And for Leonard,
his dad

I'm a teeny tiny baby

and I know how to get anything I want.

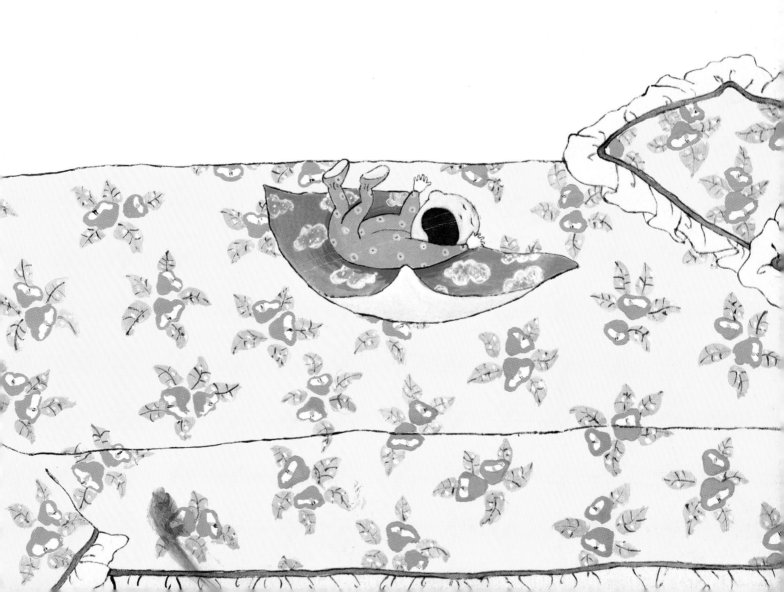

Sometimes I want to be jiggled or tickled or patted or burped

or rocked or carried

or held close.

Or sometimes
I enjoy a tour
of the apartment.

I like to be exclaimed over
and *ooh*ed over
and *ahhh*ed over,
or fed
or changed,

or sometimes
I just want
to be left
to my own devices.

or in my stroller

or in a car

Sometimes
I want to ride
in my Snugli

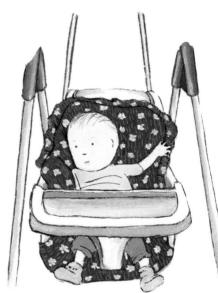

or a bus

or my swing

or my sling
or my other Snugli.

I like to go to the deli

and the cleaners

and the park

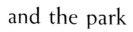

and the playground
on Pierrepont Street
or the one on Cranberry.
I've gone to the waterfront
and A&S
and to my dad's office,

and the hardware store

and the drugstore

and out for groceries.

And once I even went out for dinner.

I like to meet new people when I'm out.
"He's so little!" they say, or
"He's so big!"
"Is it a boy?" or
"Is it a girl?"

Or once a big kid stopped and said,
"He has no hair!"
Which I didn't appreciate.

And once when I was brand-new,
I went to the botanic garden
and the guard asked how old I was.
"Two weeks," Mom said.
"Ahhh," said the guard,
"and already he's seen the forsythia."

I like to eat when the sun hasn't quite risen yet
and then again when I decide to really get up
and then a little later
and then in the afternoon

and a little while before supper
and a little while after
and when the moon comes up
and a few times later in the evening,

and then again
when it's still
and dark
and me and Mom
are the only ones up.

Except for Dad.

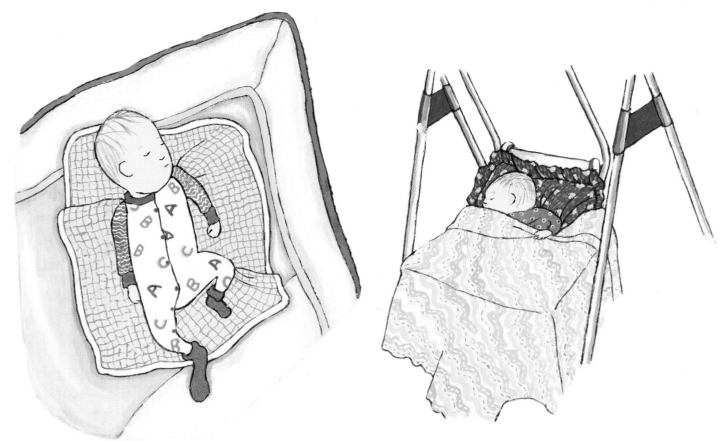

I like to sleep
on my quilt
or in my swing
or on the sofa
(though once I fell off),
or in the car

or on my sheepskin rug,
on my right side
or my left side
or on my belly
or my back.
I don't like to sleep in my cradle.
But I do like to sleep with Mom and Dad.

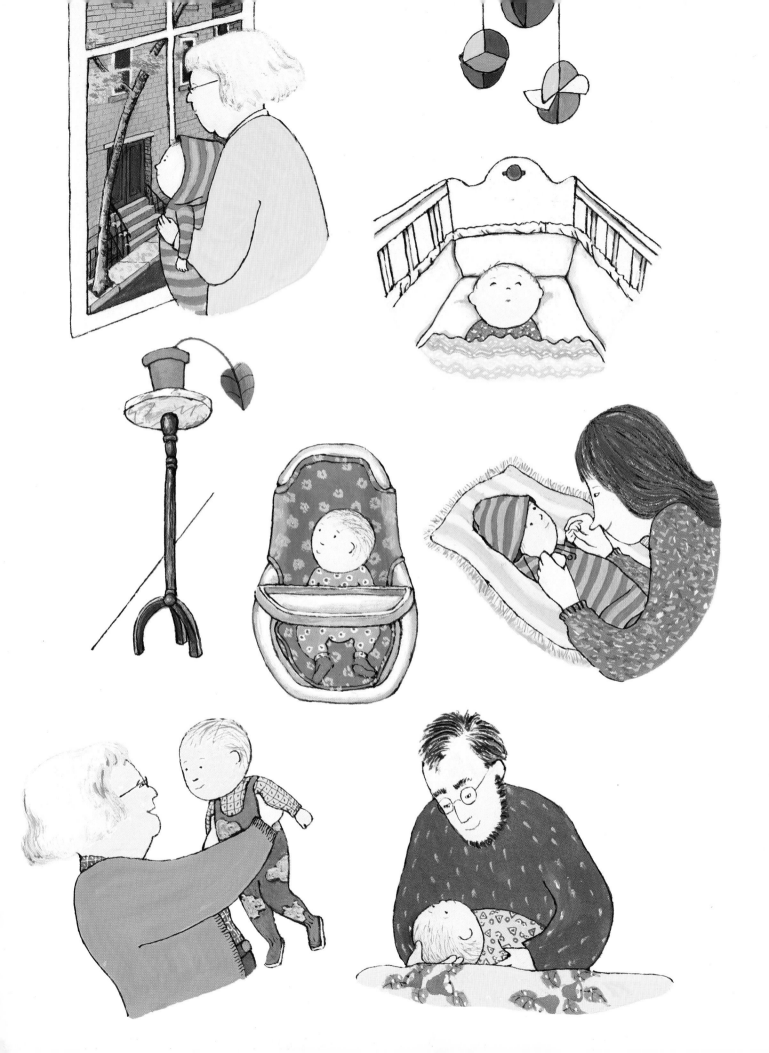

I like looking
out the window
and at my mobile
and at the plant in the living room
and at Mom's face,
or right above it,
and at Grandma's glasses
and at my dad's beard.
I also like looking
at the ceiling
and the wall
and the sky
and the trees.
I'm not very interested
in other babies,

but I do very much like
the one in the mirror.
And when we look at each other,
we always stop crying.
And then,
after we think about it,

we smile.